What Is the Weather Today?

Augustus Grayson

Infomax Readers

Rosen Classroom™

New York

Published in 2013 by The Rosen Publishing Group, Inc.
29 East 21st Street, New York, NY 10010

Book Design: Katelyn Londino

Photo Credits: Cover Allen Donikowski/Flickr/Getty Images; p. 4 JaySi/Shutterstock.com; pp. 5, 15 (snow) goran cakmazovic/Shutterstock.com; pp. 5, 15 (rain) NINA MOURIER/StockImage/Getty Images; pp. 5, 15 (sunny) Vaclav Volrab/Shutterstock.com; p. 5 (trees) © iStockphoto.com/GAPS; pp. 6, 16 (bathing suit) © iStockphoto.com/Phrysphotos; pp. 7, 14 (rain on window) © iStockphoto.com/borchee; pp. 8, 14, 15, 16 (cloudy) Anson0618/Shutterstock.com; pp. 9, 15, 16 (clear sky) © iStockphoto.com/ineskoleva; pp. 10, 14 (kite) Elinag/Shutterstock.com; p. 11 Siri Stafford/Lifesize/Getty Images; pp. 12, 14 (snowman) Gorilla/Shutterstock.com; pp. 13, 15, 16 (pool) Rocky33/Shutterstock.com.

ISBN: 978-1-4488-8968-6
6-pack ISBN: 978-1-4488-8969-3

Manufactured in the United States of America

CPSIA Compliance Information: Batch #WS12RC: For further information contact Rosen Publishing, New York, New York at 1-800-237-9932.

Word Count: 138

Contents

I know many different kinds of weather.
Weather is what it's like outside.

The weather changes every day.

It's fun to watch the weather change!

I go to the beach on a sunny day.

I wear a new bathing suit.

I stay inside on a rainy day.
It's very wet outside.

I see a gray sky on a cloudy day.

I see a blue sky when it's not cloudy.

The sky is clear.

I fly my kite in the park on a windy day.

I can't fly my kite when it's not windy.

I play ball with my friends instead.

I make a snowman on a snowy day
in the winter.
Snowy days are cold days!

I swim in the pool on a hot day.

It's hot in the summer.

What kind of weather do you have today?

Kinds of Weather

sunny

rainy

cloudy

clear

cold

hot

Words to Know

bathing suit

clear

cloudy

pool

Index